This book belongs to:

....

Copyright © 2019 Acamar Films Ltd

First published in the UK in 2016 by HarperCollins *Children's Books,*
a division of HarperCollins *Publishers* Ltd, 1 London Bridge Street, London SE1 9GF.
This edition published by HarperCollins *Children's Books* in 2019.

5 7 9 10 8 6 4

ISBN: 978-0-00-797698-0

The Bing television series is an Acamar Films production, co-produced in association with Brown Bag Films,
and adapted from the original books by Ted Dewan

Based on the script by Lead Writer Jayne Kirkham and Team Writers Lucy Murphy, Mikael Shields and An Vrombaut

Edited by Stella Gurney, Freddie Hutchins and An Vrombaut

Designed by Wayne Redwood

Looking After Flop

HarperCollins *Children's Books*

Round the corner, not far away,
Bing's just woken up today.

"Fl-op!"

"Morning Bing..."

Oh! Flop's voice
is all croaky.

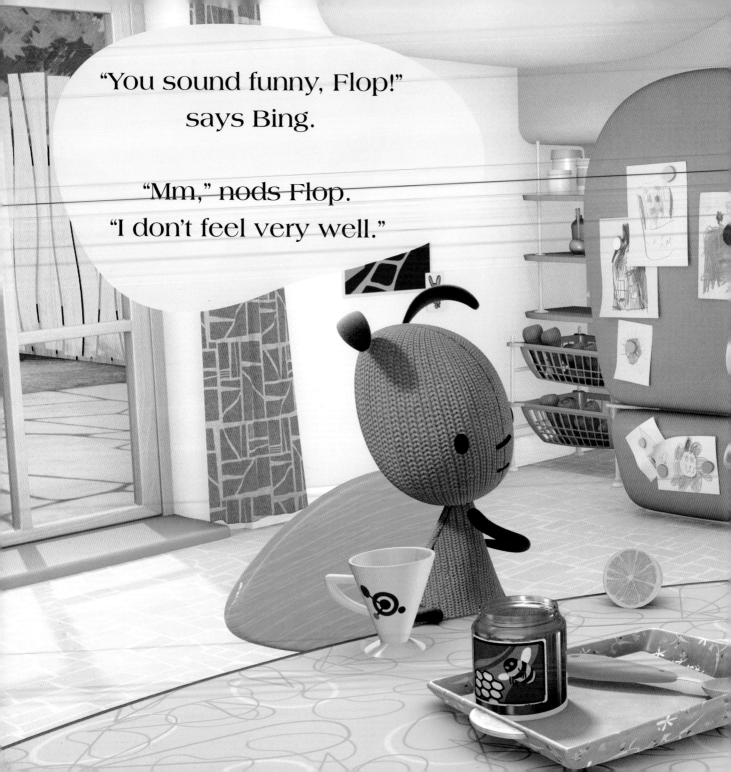

"You sound funny, Flop!"
says Bing.

"Mm," nods Flop.
"I don't feel very well."

"Why?" asks Bing.

"Well, my throat's all sore. I'm making **hot honey** and **lemon** to help it feel better."

"There," says Flop. "Hot water with a nice squeeze of lemon… and a little spoon of honey."

Poor Flop! Bing doesn't want him to feel ill.

"Oh!" Bing has an idea. "I can look after you, Flop!"

Bing takes Flop's hand and leads him to the sofa.

"You need a **cushion,** Flop.

And a **blanket.**

Oh – and **Hoppity** will make you feel better."

"Is your sore throat better **now**, Flop?" asks Bing.

"Well, not yet. It won't get better straight away, Bing."

"**Oh**," says Bing, disappointed.

"**I know!** You can have a **story**…

Hoppity Voosh and the Lonely Lettuce.

I'm going to read it to YOU,
because I'm looking after you, Flop!"

So Bing reads the story.

"Hoppity Voosh
was fast asleep...

*snore,
snore!*

Oh! Someone's crying!

*Boo
hoo
hoo!*

So Hoppity went,

voooooooosh!

And…

…look, Flop! That's the lettuce!"

Flop has closed
his eyes.

"Flop!" says Bing. "You're not listening!"

"Mm – wha–?" jumps Flop. "Oh, I am listening, Bing!"

"Are you better NOW, Flop?" asks Bing.

"Well yes," nods Flop. "I am a bit better, because I'm enjoying your story."

Oh-

a-a-a...

"Oh, Flop! You need more honey and lemon. I'll get you some!"

"Oh, don't touch the kettle Bing – it might still be hot. But I'd love some COLD water please."

Bing is in the kitchen all by himself.

He's **looking after** Flop!

He fetches his penguin cup and
fills it with cold water.

To help make Flop better, Bing adds...

some squeezy lemon

and a dribbly spoonful of honey

...and he finds an extra crunchy carrot for Flop to nibble on. Bing puts everything together on a tray.

"Coming, Flop!"

But – oh! The carrot
is all wobbly!

"Ohh – stay still, carrot!"

"Ohhhh...

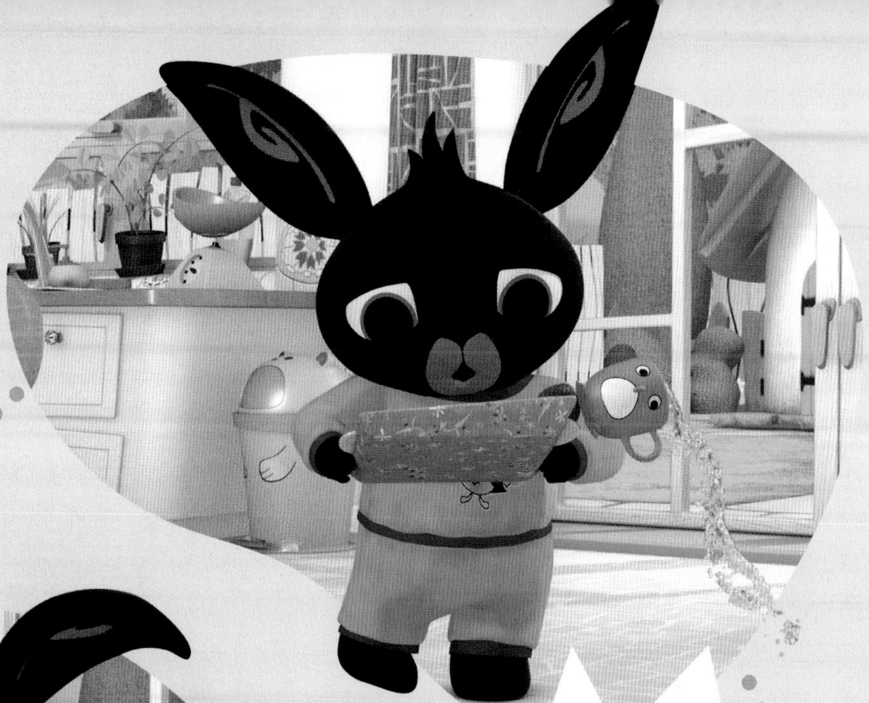

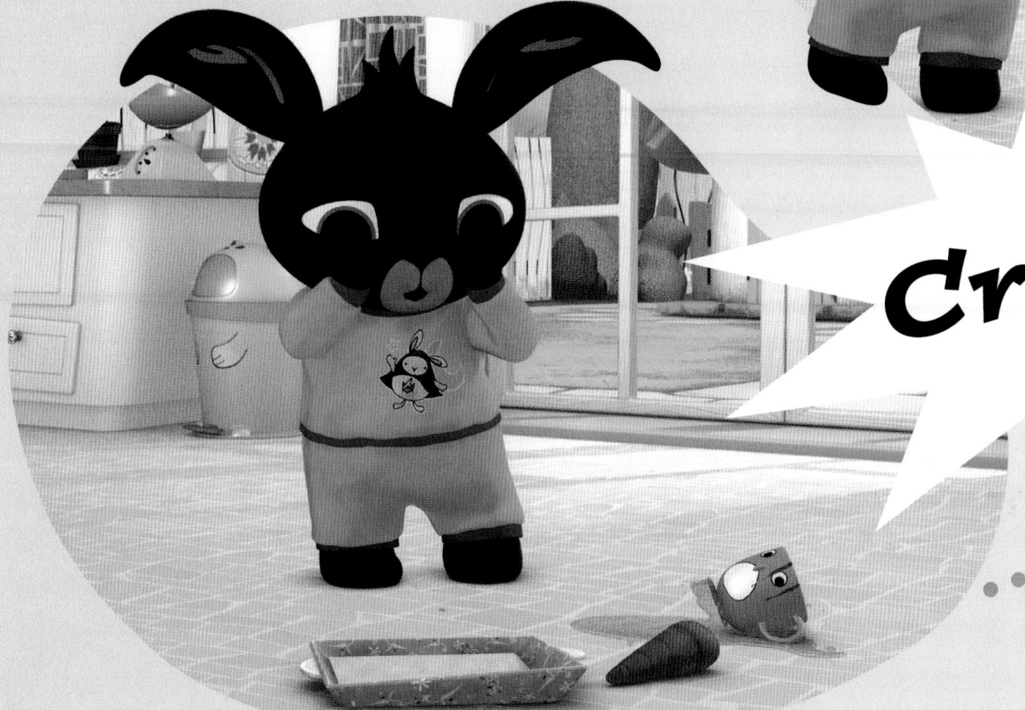

Crash!

...nooooo!"

Flop comes in.

"Are you OK, Bing?"

"**NO!**" cries Bing. "I was making
you c-cold honey and le-lemon and...
and then it all **falled over!**"

"Oh – don't worry, Bing," soothes Flop.
"It's no big thing. You've looked
after me so well."

"Come on, let's wash those sticky hands."

Bing sniffles.

"You **still** sound funny, Flop. **When** will you be better?"

"Well – it won't be **straight away**, Bing. But maybe tomorrow."

"Ohhh."

"You know, Bing," smiles Flop. "There's one thing that might make us **both feel better...**"

"What?" sniffs Bing.

"…a hug!"

"Oh! I'm good at hugs," says Bing.

"Indeed!" smiles Flop.

"Good for you, Bing Bunny."

Hi!

Flop wasn't well and he had a **sore throat** and he sounded **all funny.**

Poor Flop.

So, I looked after him!

I gave him a **cushion** and a **blanket** and **Hoppity** to help him feel better.

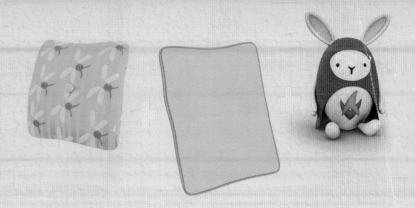

But I tried to make him a drink, and the **honey** and **lemon** and the **carrot** made a **mess**, and Flop **still** wasn't better! And I was **sad**.

I couldn't make Flop's **sore throat** go away, but we had a **hug** and **watched TV** and then we both felt better.

Looking after Flop...

it's a Bing thing.